Superstars
of the
CHICAGO
BULLS

by David Aretha

AMICUS HIGH INTEREST ✦ AMICUS INK

Amicus High Interest and Amicus Ink
are imprints of Amicus
P.O. Box 1329, Mankato, MN 56002
www.amicuspublishing.us

Library of Congress Cataloging-in-Publication Data
Aretha, David.
  Superstars of the Chicago Bulls / by David Aretha.
     pages cm. -- (Pro Sports Superstars (NBA))
  Includes index.
  Audience: Grade: K to Grade 3.
  ISBN 978-1-60753-766-3 (library binding)
  ISBN 978-1-60753-865-3 (ebook)
  ISBN 978-1-68152-017-9 (paperback)
  1. Chicago Bulls (Basketball team)--History--Juvenile literature. 2.
Basketball players--United States--Biography--Juvenile literature. I. Title.
  GV885.52.C45A74 2015
  796.323'640977311--dc23
                         2014044132

Photo Credits: Charles Cherney/AP Images, cover; Paul Abell/AP Images,
2, 18–19; Charles Rex Arbogast/AP Images, 5; Focus on Sport/Getty
Images, 6, 11, 22; Dick Raphael/NBAE/Getty Images, 8; Nathaniel S. Butler/
NBAE/Getty Images, 13, 14; Steve Lipofsky/Corbis, 16; Alex Brandon/AP
Images, 21

Produced for Amicus by The Peterson Publishing Company
and Red Line Editorial.

Designer Becky Daum

HC 10 9 8 7 6 5 4 3 2
PB 10 9 8 7 6 5 4 3 2 1

TABLE OF CONTENTS

MEET THE CHICAGO BULLS

The Chicago Bulls began in 1966. The team has won six NBA championships. It has had many stars. Here are some of the best.

BOB LOVE

Bob Love joined the Bulls in 1968. He scored many baskets. Love was a great shooter. He could shoot with both hands.

Love was nicknamed "Butterbean." He loved eating these beans.

NORM VAN LIER

Norm Van Lier was short for a basketball player. He stood about six feet tall. But he played strong defense. He had many steals. Van Lier was a top defender in 1974.

ARTIS GILMORE

Artis Gilmore was called "The A-Train." His height helped him **rebound**. He played in six **All-Star Games**. The first was in 1978.

HORACE GRANT

The Bulls picked Horace Grant in the 1987 **NBA Draft**. He joined a talented team. Grant helped out by grabbing rebounds. He won three championships with the Bulls.

SCOTTIE PIPPEN

Scottie Pippen joined the team in 1987. He was a great defender. Pippen stole the ball. He blocked shots. Pippen is in the **Basketball Hall of Fame**.

Pippen played in the Olympics. He won two gold medals.

MICHAEL JORDAN

Michael Jordan was one of the top stars ever. He hit **jump shots**. He jumped for **slam dunks**. Jordan won six championships. The last was in 1998.

Jordan once scored 69 points in one game.

DERRICK ROSE

Derrick Rose was the 2011 **MVP**.

Rose is fast. He drives to the basket.

He scores on **layups**. He is a skilled

passer too.

JOAKIM NOAH

Joakim Noah plays with energy. He leaps for rebounds. He is a quick defender. Noah played in the 2014 All-Star Game.

The Bulls have had many great superstars. Who will be next?

TEAM FAST FACTS

Founded: 1966

Home Arena: United Center in Chicago, Illinois

Mascot: Benny the Bull

Leading Scorer: Michael Jordan (29,277 points)

NBA Championships: 6 (1991, 1992, 1993, 1996, 1997, 1998)

Hall of Fame Players: 9, including Artis Gilmore, Michael Jordan, and Scottie Pippen

WORDS TO KNOW

All-Star Game – a yearly game played between the best NBA players

Basketball Hall of Fame – a museum that honors the best basketball players ever

jump shot – a shot taken after jumping in the air

layup – a one-handed shot made after leaping up from beneath the basket

MVP – Most Valuable Player; an honor given to the best player in the NBA each season

NBA Draft – a yearly event in which NBA teams choose new players, usually from college or overseas

rebound – to grab a missed shot

slam dunk – a shot in which the player jumps high and throws the ball down through the rim

LEARN MORE

Books

Frisch, Aaron. *Chicago Bulls (NBA Champions)*. Mankato, Minn.: Creative Education, 2012.

Labrecque, Ellen. *Chicago Bulls (Favorite Basketball Teams)*. North Mankato, Minn.: Child's World, 2010.

Websites

Chicago Bulls—Official Site
http://www.nba.com/bulls
Watch videos and read stories about the Chicago Bulls.

NBA.com
http://www.nba.com
Follow all the teams and players in the NBA.

NBA Hoop Troop
http://www.nbahooptroop.com
Play games and watch videos on this NBA kids site.

INDEX